The Angel Tree

A Coloring Book about Angels and Chakras

Illustrated by: Rosio Barrenachea

TRACY BLOM

Learn About Your Chakras!

- **The Crown Chakra** is located just above the top of the head, and opens upward like a funnel of energy allowing you to receive guidance, insight and wisdom. The color of this chakra is violet.

- **The Third Eye Chakra** is located just above your eyes in the center of your forehead. This chakra is where intuition, foresight, and a connection to the universe resides. The color of this chakra is indigo.

- **The Throat Chakra** is located in the center of your throat and helps you with communication, finding your voice, and self-expression. The color of this chakra is light blue.

- **The Heart Chakra** is located in the center of your chest, where compassion, love, and healing exists. The colors of this chakra are green and light pink.

- **The Solar Plexus Chakra** is located just above your navel, and is a powerful energy source in your body. Here you will find your personal power, soul's purpose, and self-love. The color of this chakra is yellow.

- **The Sacral Chakra** is located about three inches below your navel and is connected to your emotions, stability, and happiness. The color of this chakra is orange.

- **The Root Chakra** is located at the base of the spine and represents a healthy foundation for your life. This chakra connects you to the energy of Mother Earth and allows you to feel safe as you grow. The color of this chakra is red.

On a cold winter's night a little girl and her cat sat snuggly in their blankets counting snowflakes, as a bright, golden leaf blew past the window.

All of the trees in the forest were surely bare, so she went out to find the source of the golden leaf. There in the woods stood a radiant tree, unlike anything she had ever seen. "What are you?" she asked. Then something appeared

Archangel Uriel/ Root Chakra

The little girl planted her feet and stood tall, like the tree, as the Archangel Uriel spoke. "I am the bringer of nourishment, connecting to the source of all that exists. The roots of this tree provide nourishment to the whole, as I provide nourishment for your soul. Call upon me when you need help with grounding, growth, and connecting to universal wisdom."

Archangel Michael / Sacral Chakra

Orange leaves began to wrap around the base of the tree, protecting it like a mighty shield, as another angel appeared. The girl knew his name as Michael, one of God's strongest angels. "I am a clearer of darkness and a protector of peace. Call upon me when you need help removing anything that is bothering you."

MICHAEL

Sacral Chakra

Archangel Jophiel/ Solar Plexus Chakra

A beautiful angel emerged from the trees, and as the angel spoke, the girl closed her eyes. "I am Jophiel, the Archangel of art, beauty, creativity, and connecting to your soul's purpose. Call upon me when you need help expressing joy, bliss, and stepping into the flow of happiness."

Archangel Raphael / Heart Chakra

When the girl opened her eyes, another angel was there, holding a beautiful flower. "I am Archangel Raphael, and I bring you peace, healing, and love. I can provide guidance and wisdom to those who call upon me and dispel the illusion that we are separate from God."

Archangel Gabriel / Throat Chakra

Beautiful music flowed through the air as one of God's beloved messengers appeared. Gabriel is the Archangel of the throat chakra and speaking your truth. "Call upon me whenever you need help with your words and clarifying your ideas. I am always with you."

Archangel Metatron / Third Eye Chakra

A hush of peace fell upon her as another angel appeared. Metatron, one of God's most powerful Archangels, is the protector of children and helps illuminate the pathway to God. His chakra is the third eye, located in the center of the forehead.

Seraphim Angel / Crown Chakra

The Seraphim are celestial beings that bring wisdom and the light of God to the world. These mighty angels oversee all other angels. Their colors are purple and violet, and their chakra is the crown chakra, located just above the head.

SERAPHIM

Crown Chakra

Loving arms wrapped around the girl as her mother whispered in her ear. "You must have fallen asleep, my dear." She looked toward the window. "But I saw angels! They were really here!" Her mother smiled. "They always are."

The next day she returned to the forest and stood tall like the tree. She took a deep breath and imagined the colors of the angels, shining like a rainbow within, and smiled.

www.ingramcontent.com/pod-product-compliance
Lightning Source LLC
Chambersburg PA
CBHW041009170626
46815CB00002B/220